Kathryn Cave has written fiction and non-fiction for children of all ages. In 1997 she was awarded the first UNESCO Prize for Services to Tolerance in Children's Literature, for her story *Something Else* (Puffin). Among her many other titles are *Dragonrise*, *Best Friends for Ever* and *Running Battles* (all Puffin), *The Emperor's Grucklehound* and *Horatio Happened* (Hodder), and *Out for the Count* and *W is for World* (Frances Lincoln). Kathryn has worked in publishing for over 25 years and is currently Editorial Director of adult books at Frances Lincoln. She lives in London.

Terry McKenna studied at the Central School of Speech and Drama. His previous titles include *The Fox and the Circus Bear* (runner-up for the Mother Goose award), *Naughty Norman* and *What's in the Box?* (Ginn), *The Thursday Creature* (Methuen) and *The House is Haunted* (Hippo). Terry lives in Norfolk.

First published in 1989 by Windward,
under licence from Frances Lincoln Limited

This edition published in 2000 by
Frances Lincoln Limited, 4 Torriano Mews,
Torriano Avenue, London NW5 2RZ

British Library Cataloguing in Publication Data
available on request

ISBN 0-7112-0520-5 paperback

Printed in Hong Kong

1 3 5 7 9 8 6 4 2

Kathryn Cave

illustrated by
Terry McKenna

FRANCES LINCOLN

At eight o'clock on Monday morning
Tom was fast asleep and snoring.
He lay in an untidy heap,
chasing dragons in his sleep.

On the round clock, the short hand is pointing at 8 and the long hand is pointing at 12. It's 8 o'clock.

The digital clock says 8.00. That means 8 o'clock too.

At five past eight, 'Where's Tom?' Mum said.
'That lazy boy! He's still in bed.'
She put cold water in a cup
and went upstairs to wake him up.

It’s taken the long hand 5 minutes to move round to 1. The time is 5 past 8.

It’s 5 minutes since 8 o’clock so the digital clock says 8.05.

At ten past eight Tom blinked his eyes,
rubbed his hair with some surprise,
yawned and shivered, scratched his nose
and hunted round to find his clothes.

The long hand has moved on round the clock to point at 2. It's 10 past 8.

The digital clock says 8.10.

At quarter past Tom found his socks
underneath his building blocks.
He began to build a red machine
to catch the dragons in his dream.

Now the long hand is pointing at 3. It has travelled a quarter of the way round the clock. The time is a quarter past 8.

The digital clock says 8.15.

'Come on,' cried Dad. 'Enough's enough.
It's twenty past. Will you GET UP.
Your breakfast's waiting. So is mine.
I want to get to work on time.'

When the long hand
is pointing at 4 it's
20 minutes past 8.

The digital clock
says 8.20.

Tom dressed in haste, tripped on the cat
and got downstairs in nothing flat.
It was, when Mum had filled his plate,
exactly twenty-five past eight.

Another five minutes have gone by and the long hand has moved on to point at 5. It's 25 minutes past 8.

On the digital clock it says 8.25.

At half past Dad was at the door,
and Tom was busy looking for
his gym shoes, lunch box, gloves and coat,
his maths book, spellings, and his note.

The long hand has travelled halfway round the clock and the short hand is halfway between 8 and 9. It's half-past 8.

The digital clock says 8.30.

Tom found his shoes, Mum checked his maths,
Dad saved his lunch box from the cat.
At twenty-five to nine, light-hearted,
they went to get the engine started.

The long hand is pointing at 7. In 25 minutes it will be 9 o'clock. The time is 25 to 9.

The digital clock says 8.35 because it's 35 minutes since 8 o'clock.

It didn't take them very long
to see that there was something wrong.
At twenty to Dad groaned and said,
'Come on – we'll have to run instead.'

The long hand is pointing at 8. It will be 9 o'clock in 20 minutes' time so the time is 20 to 9.

The digital clock says 8.40.

With thudding hearts and pounding feet
Tom and Dad raced up the street,
puffing, panting, muscles straining.
At quarter to it started raining.

The long hand is pointing at 9.
It has travelled three-quarters
of the way around the clock.
The time is a quarter to 9.

The digital clock says 8.45.

Tom lost a glove, Dad dropped his case.
(These things can happen in a race.)
They both were running out of time
And out of breath at ten to nine.

The long hand is pointing at 10. In 10 minutes it will be 9 o'clock so the time is 10 to 9.

The digital clock says 8.50.

But there it was – the school at last!
Tom gave a shout, Dad gave a gasp.
At five to nine they reached the gate.
The school bell rang. Tom wasn't late.

The long hand is pointing at 11. In 5 minutes it will be 9 o'clock. The time is 5 to 9.

The digital clock says 8.55.

At nine o'clock on Monday morning
Tom found class work rather boring.
Instead of handing crayons round
he called a passing dragon down.
They soar high up above the mist
to lands where time does not exist.

The long hand is pointing straight up at 12 again, and the short hand is pointing at 9. The time is 9 o'clock.

The digital clock says 9.00. That means 9 o'clock too.

TELLING THE TIME

In every hour there are 60 minutes. You can see them marked out around the edge of the round clock on this page.
The long hand tells the minutes, and it takes an hour to move all the way round the clockface. When the long hand is on its way from the 12 to the 6 we give the time in minutes past the hour, such as, 25 past 8. But once the long hand passes the number 6, we give the time in minutes before the hour, so we don't say 35 past 8, but 25 to 9.
The short hand tells the hour. It moves round the clockface too, but it takes 12 hours to go all the way round, one hour for each number.
You need to look at both the long and the short hands to see what time the clock says.

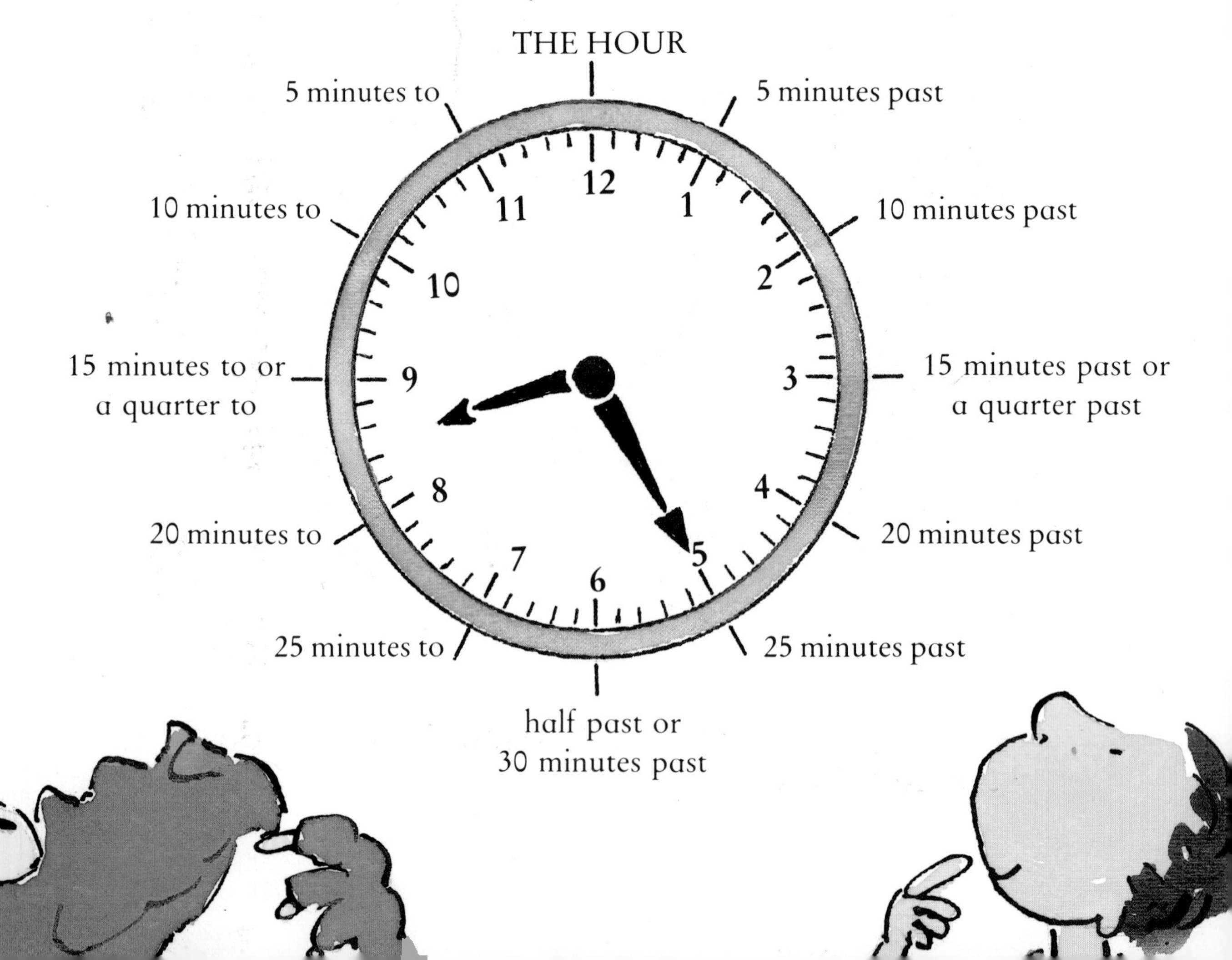

On a digital clock, the first number is the hour, then there is a dot or two dots followed by the number of minutes past the hour. The second number can't be more than 59 minutes because there are only 60 minutes in an hour, and the next time after 11:59 will be 12:00, not 11:60!

Can you match the times on the round clocks with the times on the digital clocks?